TRANSITION
TALES
Stories for the Great Turning

Jessie Darlington

BALBOA.
PRESS

A DIVISION OF HAY HOUSE

This is a work of fiction. All of the characters, names, incidents, organizations, and dialogue in this novel are either the products of the author's imagination or are used fictitiously.

Balboa Press books may be ordered through booksellers or by contacting:

Balboa Press
A Division of Hay House
1663 Liberty Drive
Bloomington, IN 47403
www.balboapress.com
1 (877) 407-4847

Because of the dynamic nature of the Internet, any web addresses or links contained in this book may have changed since publication and may no longer be valid. The views expressed in this work are solely those of the author and do not necessarily reflect the views of the publisher, and the publisher hereby disclaims any responsibility for them.

The author of this book does not dispense medical advice or prescribe the use of any technique as a form of treatment for physical, emotional, or medical problems without the advice of a physician, either directly or indirectly. The intent of the author is only to offer information of a general nature to help you in your quest for emotional and spiritual well-being. In the event you use any of the information in this book for yourself, which is your constitutional right, the author and the publisher assume no responsibility for your actions.

Any people depicted in stock imagery provided by Thinkstock are models, and such images are being used for illustrative purposes only. Certain stock imagery © Thinkstock.

Print information available on the last page.

ISBN: 978-1-5043-9495-6 (sc)
ISBN: 978-1-5043-9496-3 (e)

Balboa Press rev. date: 03/07/2018

Dedication

For all you story tellers who are busy weaving the fabric of a new heaven and a new earth.

Acknowledgements

A heartfelt thank you to <u>all</u> those shambhala warriors who have been a lifelong inspiration to myself and so many others in dark and uncertain times. There are too many to name them all. Thank you for stories of hope and sign posts suggesting which path to take. Thank you to the ever attentive and patient inner teacher and guide. And finally, thank you to those special close ones who are sharing the story this time round, Andy, Robin and Jeremy.

Transition Tales; Stories for the '*Great Turning*'

In 2006 a permaculture teacher called Rob Hopkins started a movement in the town of Totnes in southern England which he chose to call 'transition'* [1].

He wanted to find ways of collectively changing the story we are in. He wanted it to be a story of hope rather than a tragedy. It was not a story that ignored the mess we are in. Instead it looked at the situation we have created, everything from diminishing resources, climate change, economic crisis and population explosion, and tried to find ways of turning a big problem into an amazing resource. It was a story we would rewrite together; a product of our collective creativity.

The stories we share have a major impact on our perception of reality. They build cultures. Looking at what stories we tell and how we can purposefully choose to tell different ones is a good way to begin making important changes in our world.

I once listened to renowned author Jean Houston share an experience from her childhood. She told of a visit to see Albert Einstein with her class in primary school. When asked by one child -

"How can we become as intelligent as you?", he apparently replied,

"Read more fairy tales!"

He understood the importance of fostering the imagination. Our imaginations help us to build the future scenarios we want to see enacted in our world.

The few stories I have chosen to share here were seminal for my own understanding and sense of hope for the future, but this book is also an invitation; an invitation to curl up by the fire and listen to the deep silence of the void where it all begins. Listen to the voice within you that whispers the story of a future that we can consciously choose. This is the challenge that I would like to share with you here and these tales may just be the beginning of a long night of storytelling that precedes the dawn of a new era. Stories of courage and heroism, of tenderness and compassion, stories that encourage and inspire, old stories retold with new relevance, new stories discovered, things that we have experienced or tales we have heard from others to help us through the darkest hours and see beyond them. They are stories that use all the wisdom of the past and all the wonderful discoveries of our times to invent the future.

Story telling was once the domain of the shaman or medicine man, simply because those were the people who could imagine something unseen and share their vision with the rest of the tribe.

Nowadays we all share some of those attributes; we can all imagine a different story in our minds eye and share it with others. When we learn to speak or write in any language – when we learn to share our story- we gain a kind of access to power. Until we develop that faculty, our silence is taken as acquiescence to someone else's story, a story that might not always be in everyone's best interest.

The sharing part is important too, because when we really manage to share a dream with others they can make it their dream as well. They add something of themselves to it by making it their own and it increases in richness and power. The story form also gives us heroes or models of behaviour that we can emulate and aspire to. It leaves us with an image of where we are headed so that we can be there before we arrive, because that is how the physical world we live in becomes manifest. So let us set to and tell a story really worth bringing into reality.

Shambhala Warriors* (3)

Jessie Darlington

When I was nearing the end of high school my father asked me what I wanted to do with my life. I told him that most of all, I wanted to change the world and he replied, like someone that no longer believed such a thing was realistic, that he too, had dreamt of doing that once. However, now our world really is in grave danger; after 10 thousand years of gathering intensity, humanity's rape of the earth is out of control and our destiny hangs in the balance. Abandoning our faith in our ability to change is no longer an option.

All beings in the web of life feel this imminent danger through the shimmering threads that connect them to each other and to the whole of nature, of which we are a part. Yes, even we humans who seem to have cut ourselves off from other living creatures, have a deep sense that there is a danger lurking that we cannot always identify.

Our reaction is often one of fear and our attempt to protect ourselves from the invisible danger divides us into 'goodies' and 'baddies'. We invent conspiracy theories, dive into virtual realities, build more walls and barbed wire fences, impose rules and restrictions, attempt to 'eliminate bacteria', and employ more and more repressive armed forces to protect ourselves.

In the midst of this growing chaos there are 'warriors' who carry a new heaven and a new earth like a flame in their hearts and minds. Ancient prophecies tell of their coming. They are warriors without uniforms or even countries as we would imagine. They have skins of many colours and wear different garbs. Some are young, others old and still others are being born as we speak. Their numbers grow daily and they are fearless because they have chosen to come at this time in earth's history. You will not find them defending positions or dropping bombs but rather in the walks of everyday life, some in lowly places others in the corridors of power where prime ministers and presidents make decisions. They might be taking part in corporate meetings with business magnates or down a sewer that hides some homeless people in the entrails of a city. Wherever they find themselves they work quietly to dismantle the mind-made evil that threatens all of life.

These warriors work alone. They know that all 'evil' comes from inside and that it cannot be fought with weapons of mass destruction. There are no 'bad guys' and 'good guys' because good and evil coexist in each of us. They understand that there is no 'enemy' other than our own fear and greed, that this is a struggle that will be won internally through self-awareness, through individual choices based on each soul's commitment to the web of life.

They are learning how to use the two most powerful forces that exist – compassion and insight. Compassion burns like a fire in a dark night and gives them the strength to go forward and work for an end to suffering with a warm heart. Insight runs through them like a cool stream at midday, clearing head and eyes, helping them to understand that all beings suffer, that all air is the same air, that all water is the same water, that the earth is our body and that all good, however small, serves the common good. They know that 'evil' is mind-made and can therefore be 'unmade'.

Make havens for these warriors to rest in. Learn how to use these gifts. Perhaps you too are such a warrior and life waits for your coming with short anxious breaths.

The Two Wolves

This story is told by the Cherokee Indians to their children but really it is the story of every man, woman, and child on the planet. I have retold it here because I believe that it is of fundamental importance to our understanding of where our power lies.

A tribal elder told his young listeners across the fire;

"There are two wolves that live inside of me and they are always fighting.

One hides and waits for his chance to catch the other off guard; this one is the wolf of selfishness, greed, fear, jealousy, doubt and separation. The second is the wolf of loving kindness, compassion, joy in the joy of others, equanimity, courage, and understanding.

As soon as I begin to think, there they are, each one determined to be the one I listen to. As soon as I am asked my opinion they snarl and snark, wrestling with each other for the space. Whenever I must make a choice, the two of them are there waiting and the battle starts... and when I go to take action, they begin again."

"And which one do you think will win?" asked the children, intrigued.

"That, my dears, is simple," said the old man. "It will be the one I feed! But watch out, for these two wolves live in each of us and if you are paying attention, you will meet them inside of yourself every day! Be careful to feed only the wolf of loving kindness, that your thoughts, words and deeds may obey his council. That way, the wolf of selfishness, greed and hatred will become weaker and weaker and you will live in peace."

Which wolf are you feeding and what do you feed him with? Mass media, vendettas, quarrels, scandal, propaganda, scapegoating, gossip, competitiveness and fundamentalism all help to nourish the wolf of fear and separation. This produces feelings of 'they are different from us'.

On the other hand, deep listening, cultural exchange, sharing, communication, voluntary community service and self-development all foster and feed the wolf of loving kindness and compassion. They help us reconnect with each other and the web of life 'of which we are only a thread' *[4]*

Sowing the seeds of peace

Ismael and his wife Abia lived in the Jenin refugee camp on the narrow strip of land known as the 'West Bank' in the dry, sun-baked country of Palestine. Ismael had to travel to Israel every day to work in a mechanic's workshop.

Water was scarce, as were medical supplies. Even food was often short on the West Bank. There were many who had to go and look for work in neighbouring Israel and Ismael spent long hours every day in queues of traffic and at border check points. He was lucky to have a job.

Often there was the sound of gunfire. Always there was anger, hatred, despair; too many people on too little land, hemmed in by rolls of barbed wire and walls built out of bricks and fear. This was not the future that Ismael and Abia wished for their six children, four boys and two girls, growing up so fast in what was really a war zone.

It all started on the first day of the Muslim festival of Eid el Fior. Twelve-year-old Ahmed Khatib, the third eldest, was up early helping his mother in the kitchen. Then he dressed proudly in his new clothes to go to the mosque and visit the martyrs graveyard, where the men killed in the 'intifada' or war of liberation were buried.

Since Ahmed had grown up in the refugee camp he had taken as models those fighters of the Al Aqua Martyrs' Brigade, men who defiantly resisted Israeli occupation. When he was only nine he had seen the whole center of the refugee camp destroyed by the Israeli army leaving many dead and wounded. His whole world consisted of that closely hemmed-in camp and so he emulated the behaviour of his heroes, playing with a plastic gun, leaping over piles of rubble, creeping round walls to throw stones at Israeli tanks, imagining how he and his friends would take back by force the land that had been taken from them. He collected posters of his heroes. His mother, fearful of reprisals, threw them away again.

Later on that same morning, the children heard that the Israeli army was again in the camp looking for the al Aqua Martyrs' Brigade and they set out to look for the jeeps. By the time they had found them, Ahmed was brandishing a plastic gun that looked only too real to a nervous soldier. It happened very quickly. Two bullets exploded inside Ahmed, one in his head and one in his pelvis. The other boys fled to tell Abia.

Ahmed was rushed to hospital and then to Haifa in a desperate attempt to save his life. The doctors kept his heart beating for two days, but the damage was too great and he died of his wounds. Everywhere there were people lying waiting between life and death for an organ donation that could prolong and improve the quality of their lives. So when it became obvious that Ahmed would not survive, the Israeli doctors asked Ismael and his wife if they would be willing to donate the boy's organs.

This was a difficult decision for them because the story between the people of Palestine and the tribes of Israel is a thorny and ancient one. Long ago these two peoples descended from two half-brothers, Ismael and Isaac, sons of Abraham. Over the centuries, rights to land, different religious rites and jealousy, kindled conflict. These days, both sides ignore their common origins and shared faults. They forget that their fates are inseparably woven together. Slowly, as the generations nurture the wolf of separation and jealousy inside themselves, even the land beneath their feet has grown sterile with the poison of hatred.

Sometimes extreme pain can trigger a different kind of response. If the right influences have been fostered, the wolf of loving kindness is fed, then a small ray of light can slide into the great darkness and show us a different road to take. It requires compassion, understanding that all beings suffer, and the insight to understand that more pain will not cure insufferable pain. It also requires great courage on the part of individuals to resist peer pressure, when they fear their actions may be condemned.

Ismael had spent fifteen years of his young life giving blood to one of his brothers who needed a kidney transplant and who finally died without getting a donor organ. He understood the painful reality such people experience. He also worked with Israelis in ordinary everyday life and knew that they were human beings like himself. Ismael and Abia decided to give their son's body parts to six Israeli children, four of them of the Jewish faith – 'children of the enemy'.

A little Jewish girl called Samedh was given Ahmed's heart. She had suffered for five years with a genetic heart disease, the same disease her brother had died from. Samedh's mother knew the pain of losing a son.

When asked by a reporter what had given him the courage to do such a thing, Ismael replied:

"I am sowing the seeds of peace in the children of my enemy."

This story reminds us that in spite of all our seemingly irreconcilable differences, there are more things that we share than things that we do not. We all seek happiness, to be free of sorrow. We all love our children and hope for peace. We all need healthy food. The same sun shines down on us and death ultimately awaits us all. When we have the presence of mind to remember this, our fear dissolves and we are one again. Each time someone manages to respond to their own suffering by reaching out with compassion, they make a bridge to a new kind of reality, a bridge that others may cross over.

How the wild Geese Fly

Every winter wild geese gather in the far north of America to make the grueling journey south for the winter. They have fed on the autumn fruits and grasses to strengthen themselves, for the journey is long and dangerous.

Perhaps you have seen their familiar flight formation in an autumn sky, long trailing V- shapes of honking, flapping birds. When they fly like this, the leader makes a pathway through the air which the other geese can fly in. This makes it easier for the birds behind to fly, as there is 70% less wind resistance. Each one follows the 'ripple' in the air in the wake of the goose in front, just like the wake made by ducks or boats passing through water. The geese at the back call out to encourage the leader to keep up the momentum. You can hear them honking as they fly. Because it is a very strenuous job being the first goose in the V-formation, the geese take it in turns to be the leader, preparing a flight path for the others.

Occasionally you will see very small groups of geese, just three or four birds on their own. They may be catching up with their flock after a few days' rest. This happens when one of the birds has been wounded or is too tired or ill to fly. Several geese accompany this member of the flock so that it can rest. They will stay in one place until that bird has recovered or died, before rejoining the flock once more on the long journey south.

We too can 'fly' like this. When one of us has the courage and inspiration to forge a new pathway, it makes it much easier for all the others to follow in the wake. We can take turns to play that leadership role; each one of us has qualities and ways of leading that are appropriate at different moments and in different circumstances. When that role has been fulfilled, we can step aside gracefully and let another person take over. Pooling our resources in this way we are all stronger. Only deep recognition of our inter-dependence or 'interbeing'*[5], will allow us to go beyond our individual agendas and to realise that some things can only be accomplished together.

The Mad PeasantWoman

This strange and wonderful story came to me from an unknown source. It was a few sentences in a conversation about our capacity to change our world by changing our own head space. Do we wear tinted lenses when we look at the world, and how does that change the way that we experience reality? Despite not knowing whether the events recounted had really happened, I nevertheless felt that the story demonstrated exciting possibilities.

It shows how all experiential reality begins with a dream, a vision or an intention. This vision makes a kind of trail in the ether which others can follow in – a bit like the geese flying in the slipstream of the lead goose. Our world transforms as we transform our understanding, dreams, and intentions.

This is the tale of one small miracle that happened during the Chernobyl disaster in 1986. In April of that year the reactor #4 of the Chernobyl power plant in the Ukraine exploded and caught fire, following a series of routine tests that went terribly wrong.

A small modern city, Pripyat, had mushroomed around the power plant to accommodate the people who worked there, but it was also surrounded by farms and fields and small villages where rural and peasant life continued much as it had for centuries.

There lived in one such village, a peasant woman who was considered by her neighbours to be quite mad, perhaps because of her excess of mystical zeal or flights of fancy. Such people have always existed. In simple peasant cultures they may be accepted as benignly crazy, adulated as was the child of Lourdes or, burnt at the stake for witchcraft because of the fear and incomprehension they provoke. In this case the woman was tolerated and her pursuit of union with her source proved to be her salvation.

Hopefully everyone now knows the sad chain of events that followed the nuclear accident. There were days of fire-fighting heroics to extinguish the blaze so that the explosion did not go further into the reactor. Thousands of citizens were evacuated. Many had already received massive doses of radiation. There was much heroic work done by soviet volunteers trying to clean up the uncleanable mess. They were to become some of the thousands who ended up ill or dying from radiation in the years that followed. Children, as well as the young of wild and domestic animals, were and continue to be born irreparably damaged. The accident also led to the pollution of all food sources and the displacement of huge swathes of population from some of the most fertile and productive farmland in northern Europe. Radioactivity continues to spread through food, wind, air, water and even recycled metal.

Unlike her neighbours, our peasant woman registered no measurable damage from the ambient radioactivity. When the power plant exploded on the 26ᵗʰ of April this woman believed that the explosion she was seeing was happening inside of her consciousness and that she had finally attained enlightenment. The effect was a bit like pushing a button; a button she must have come upon quite by accident. It had a very unusual effect on her.

This does not make radioactivity any less dangerous. Nor do we all know how to find that button, if indeed it exists. What it does show is how critical our inner state can be to the way we weather and experience great suffering and change. Author and researcher Gregg Braden has explained the mechanism that makes this possible;

"In order to change our reality we must change (with intention) the commands of feeling, emotion, prayer and belief that program reality." *(6)

They must become reality on the inside (in our sensation) before they can become reality in matter (the outside). We must change our beliefs before we can change what we project into the world. This is perhaps one of the most important things we can do, and only we can do it. No one can do it for us.

The Termites dance

Working and living together in a harmonious way has always been a challenge for human beings. It both entices and eludes us. Over the past few thousand years all our systems have tended to be designed on hierarchical patterns of power and domination rather than cooperation - the proverbial 'power over' rather than the 'power with'. And yet we have another blueprint within our psyches that we remember with longing, and try in a bumbling and clumsy way to reproduce.

In the African savannah the sun beats down relentlessly. The wind swirls the dust into hot clouds that bite the skin. Plants and animals have made this harsh country their home and they have learned over time to live with the difficult conditions and thrive. Here some of the smallest creatures live in communities of one to two million inhabitants. They are the termites.

They build termite houses to protect themselves and their brood from extreme heat and drought, as well as predators. These houses are bigger, compared to the size of a termite, than any structure that humans have built on the earth. (For us to compete with them, our houses would have to be a mile high.) They rise up like miniature skyscrapers above the ground and continue down into the earth for several meters. They have sophisticated air conditioning systems, chambers for growing mushroom cultures (a bit like market gardening) nurseries for termite young and a special room for the egg-laying termite queen. It is a complex and highly organised living space. The termite houses are made from mud; they are several stories high with vaulted ceilings and perfect arches. They go down far enough into the earth to reach the humidity of the water table. The cooling system draws the damp air up from below by means of the chimney structure above the ground level to keep the air fresh and the temperature at 31 degrees Centigrade. Scientists studying the termites have found to their surprise that they have no plans, no architects, no termite bosses telling everyone what to do. The termites are simply responding collectively to a situation of survival, instinctively knowing that their future depends on cooperation and individual initiative on behalf of the group. The termite workers bump into each other, find something that needs doing and then do it or help to do it. Their dance is a magnificent illustration of what all self-organising systems do.

Humans have the same capacity and demonstrate similar social behaviour in times of crisis, such as earthquakes or other natural disasters. Something switches on and we forget to be competitive, self-cherishing and complicated. We simply work for the common good, find access to unknown internal resources, perform heroics to save lives, draw on the power of our inter-connectedness and find even greater strength, ingenuity and joy in the face of hardship and suffering.

In fact, all of the web of life is engaged in a similar dance to that of the termites; the dance of living systems in which symbiosis, or mutual cooperation to enhance survival and living conditions, is paramount.

Scientists initially believed that plants and animals competed for space and resources. It is becoming apparent that this is not quite the whole picture. The pattern can also be described in a different way. All living beings fill complementary and temporary 'niches', gracefully finding the most appropriate place to grow and preparing the ground for the next 'guild' or community of species to arrive. All species help to control each other's excesses with short feedback loops so that they are in a constant state of dynamic movement, a bit like dancing. For example, too many wild sheep are controlled by wolves or wild cats eating the weak and diseased ones. Trees in a forest have even been shown to provide other trees with all the necessary requirements for survival when water, nutrients and even sunlight are in short supply for certain individuals. Weeds rush in to cover and protect the bare earth that has been exposed to the harsh sun, beating rains and drying winds. Humans in tribal groups make small holes in the rainforest canopy bringing light and space between the trees so that different kinds of plants can find their favourite living conditions. It is an endless, weaving dance of cooperation, listening, finding a balance, feedback, finding the balance again.

At our best, we are part of this elegant dance. It requires our full attention and deep listening, so that we don't pull our fellow dancers off balance. In this dance there is no 'boss' calling the moves. As humans we have what is called 'self-reflective consciousness' – that is we can stand back and choose. We do this as individuals but we are not necessarily able to do it yet on behalf of the collective. Yet our future survival will depend on how well we learn to dance together, sharing what we have, asking for what we need and including all the dancers in the dance.

"The next Buddha may be a *sangha*" (a community) *(7)

'Everything Gardens'

Many of the world's great religions conceive of Paradise as a garden. In the collective subconscious it is an image that many people can relate to as a place of great beauty and peace. It is also a place of bountiful harvests, a place of nourishment, food for body and soul.

When Bill Mollison, one of the originators of the Permaculture movement said, 'everything gardens' he was referring to the fact that all animals participate in maintaining the ecosystem that feeds them and of which they are a part, in a way which could be described as gardening. Humans can learn to use these gardening skills to enhance or inspire their own gardening efforts.

Equally as miraculous as the termites with their underground mushroom culture are the bears of Kazakhstan and their apple forests. In a place called Almaty, which may be roughly translated as 'the father of all apples' or the original birthplace of the apple tree, bears have been responsible for planting apple forests.

Bear has a big appetite. He can eat the entire harvest of one apple tree in a single meal …. and of course he will choose the sweetest juiciest apples just as you or I would. What he then does is deposit all those undigested apple pips that have gone through his digestive tract in a nutritious bed of bear droppings. This is just like a pre-prepared bundle of seeded compost all ready to grow into more apple trees. Many more of bear's favourite fruit will grow successfully into new trees than other less favoured apples because of this process.

What Bear has done over centuries is very like what peasant farmers have always done and what, nowadays, plant engineers also do. He has selected varieties of apple that suit his tastes and favoured their reproduction over all others.

This genetic selection has been a long gradual process but it has resulted in disease-free apples, large and sweet, that grow in natural forests together with other native species of tree. (Nature does not tend to produce monocultures (cultures of one single species)).

It has been suggested that plants will respond to the particular nutritional needs of their animal gardeners by incorporating information gathered from the gardeners' genetic makeup. They do this with the help of bacteria. Certain bacteria can actually modify DNA, or rather change the potential expression of the DNA, by bringing in new information which the plant absorbs. Perhaps passing apple pips through their digestive tracts is a way for the bears to cleverly adapt the new apple trees to their own special needs. They are turning their food into medicine for future generations.

Whales also garden in a very sophisticated way. You may have heard that plants like music and that they even have particular tastes in music, responding more favourably to certain composers. Often they like music which resembles birdsong, perhaps because of the number of notes per bar or the harmonics. Well, deep in the ocean when Mother Whale is close to the moment when she will deliver her calf, Father Whale 'sings' special songs, a kind of haunting whale music that scientists have been able to record. What they didn't know when they first noticed this pattern was that Father Whale was actually gardening! Certain whale songs or frequencies of sound cause the phytoplankton, those microscopic plants that the whales eat, to respond with better growth and higher nutritional content. In this way, Mother Whale has the abundance of the high quality food that she needs to produce milk for her calf.

Humans have learned from this experience that they can also garden with sound and get better results. If they produce similar frequencies next to their growing vegetables at particular times of the day, the plants respond with better growth and higher nutritional qualities.

These are just two of the ways in which animals maintain their food growing landscape. They are energy efficient and harmless to the overall functioning of their ecosystem. The earth is indeed a garden of paradise. One day we will abandon our destructive agricultural practices and learn to cultivate earth's garden with a natural grace and harmlessness similar to that of the animals. We will also bring intention and full awareness to the act.

Noah's Ark

Other ages have existed, other times of turmoil and upheaval. They have left no remnants behind for us to bear witness to their passing. Sometimes stories find their way down through the ages to help us humans remember in our short lives those longer cycles that make up the earths story. Noah's Ark is one such a tale.

It happened at a time when men were giants and could live to the ripe old age of nine hundred years old! It happened at a time when the world was also in danger, when humans had forgotten their place in the web of life and there was great violence in the world. Noah was one man, so the story tells us, who listened to the wisdom of his heart which some call 'God'. The voice of his heart came to him, warning,

"Humans have fallen on evil ways and will bring great destruction upon themselves and all of life."

The voice gave him very precise instructions. He was to build an ark, a kind of covered boat. It was to be built of gopher wood, painted with pitch, three hundred cubits long, fifty cubits wide, and thirty cubits high. It should be three stories high and have several rooms, one small window and a door in the side.

In this way Noah could save his family from destruction, as well as one male and one female of all living creatures. When the disaster was over they would repopulate the earth. So Noah and his sons set about building such an ark to the amusement and ridicule of all those around them. When it was finished they gathered together males and females of all species, as well as provisions to feed them, and brought them aboard.

Shortly after, the heavens opened and it began to rain. It rained, we are told, for no less than forty days and forty nights, without stopping. Every centimetre of dry land was submerged and all the beasts that could not survive in water drowned, for the flood remained on the earth for one hundred and fifty days. When at last the waters began to subside, the ark came to ground on the mountains of Ararat.

From the small window in the ark, Noah sent out a raven one day and later a dove, to determine whether there was any dry land. Both returned to the ark. The second time the dove brought back an olive branch in reply to his question. Released seven days later again, the dove did not return at all. Then Noah knew there was enough dry land again for them all to be able to leave the ark.

Then the story tells us that the voice reassured Noah and a rainbow appearing in the sky was seen as a promise that never again would all of life be destroyed by a flood.

There are many aspects of this story which make it an important reminder for us at this time in history. Once again, as an insidious man-made destruction eats away at the web of life, habitats are destroyed, plants and animals die from pollution, climate change and radioactivity. We are assailed with images of birds dead with their bellies full of plastic debris from the ocean; polar bears starving because the polar ice cap has melted and they can no longer hunt; whales and dolphins beached by radar interference; seeds patented and owned by a few who control and manipulate them for personal gain, leaving thousands to pay or starve. Slowly we are awakening not only to our role in this destruction but also to the awareness that it is a part of ourselves we are destroying. This story reminds us that for our survival it is not enough to save our own skins; that without all the millions of companions that share the earth with us, from the smallest unicellular organisms to the giants of the plant and animal kingdom, there is no life that can exist as we know it.

Some of us remember Noah and, like him, work quietly to save the miracle of plant and animal diversity as best we can. There are little Noah's arks all over the world. Many work to save the bees, to set up reserves where wild animals can rest and reproduce, create feeding stations for starving or damaged birds, save heritage seed collections, old varieties of fruit trees or disappearing races of domestic animals. And still we need more Noahs.

Maybe you too are a Noah.

What can I do?

A strange story is told of Columbus's arrival in the West Indies in which the natives were, at first, unable to see the European ships. Perhaps they had no reference from which to understand their possible existence. The shaman however had noticed a difference in the habitual wave patterns as the water lapped around the prows of the sailing vessels. This allowed him to 'see' the boats and he was then able to share his vision of another reality with the rest of the tribe.

As farfetched as this may seem, it illustrates the fact that there is much more to 'see' than we are normally aware of and that observing unusual patterns can help us widen our perspectives. It also reminds us that what has always been a reality for shamans, namely the understanding that *the world is what we think it is*, has now been proven by quantum physics to be true.

The arrival of television has increased the image-creating faculty of every human and most people can and do run their own films through their minds on a daily basis. We make very poor use of this faculty, falling prey to images and thoughts created by others, recreating negative images and scenarios rather than controlling our thoughts and directing them to positive images and outcomes. Understanding the power of our projected thought on the world we are supposedly 'observing' is vitally important. If our thoughts change, if our way of looking changes, it follows that the world, of which we are a part, will also start to change.

One of the most formative stories of my own childhood was my first visit to the cinema to watch Julie Andrews as Mary Poppins. The scene I remember most often is the one where the children present their father with a list of requirements for their new nanny, only to have it ripped up and thrown into the fireplace. Of course it didn't stop there and a puff of wind was enough to blow it up the flue and into the waiting hands of Mary Poppins herself as she drifted past under her umbrella. Minutes later she was at the door ready to fulfill all the requirements of the children's request; a strong image of manifestation to imprint on a six-year-old.

Years later, on the advice of our first permaculture teacher, my future husband and I set about imagining what the land for our permaculture project would be like. We chose a special place, a sacred place, and built ourselves a little model in the earth carefully adding all the different elements that we hoped it would include. It took a little longer to appear than Mary Poppins had done, but sure enough one year later there it was, an almost perfect replica!

Myths and stories help us to reframe a 'paradigm' or pattern of thinking for the structure and functioning of a society that must change its world view if it is to survive this difficult age. We need hope and encouragement for what Joanna Macy speaker and Buddhist philosopher, has called 'the great turning', or the changes that the new paradigm will require us to make.

I invite you to add stories you have invented or heard, of positive transformation and grace that inspire and give hope. Our imagination has been given to us so that we can envisage and build a 'new heaven and a new earth'.

Taking action is important. It is a bit like building the story in real time. Yet so often we hear a despairing, "What can I do?" as we are left feeling powerless and confused at the immensity of the problems we see around us.

Systems theory has shown us that in all systems, from atoms to far off galaxies, it is the smallest elements of the system that induce change. In society the smallest element is the individual. Contrary to what we might sometimes *feel*, the power is truly in our hands.

However, we are not alone in our concern for the state of the world and when we join together to actively participate in making the changes that are necessary, we also join forces with a power and a magic far greater than we can imagine. There are many things we can do individually as well as collectively. Here are a few ideas that can start you off. The first three were originally formulated by Bill Mollison, one of the originators of the Permaculture movement. I have added a fourth.

1) **Reduce your overall consumption, especially of non-renewables.**

Join a '*transition*' group in your town or start one of your own, in order to connect up with local networks and resources. (*Transition* is a worldwide citizen's movement that sets out to reclaim our collective power as a collaborative society, taking responsibility for food, transport, health care, education and the environment at a local level.)

Find out about and use alternative routes to mass market consumption like free-cycle, handmade, homemade, local, repair and re-use, trading systems, local currency or green money systems

Practice voluntary simplicity, or, as Gandhi said, "Live simply so that others can simply live."

2) <u>Reconnect to nature's growing cycle</u>

Work in community gardens or learn to nurture earth's garden with a good gardener. For thousands of years our main connection with nature has been through some form of gardening. All animals practice gardening in one form or another as it links them to their ecosystem and helps ensure the food supply for them and their descendants. This connectedness with nature is also a vital aspect of a healthy human community.

Grow your own food as much as possible or participate in a community supported agriculture system in your area. If you are in an inner city area you can start up a city garden with neighbours and perhaps local council support.

Go 'WWOOFing' or volunteering in a global network of organic farms. World Wide Opportunities on Organic Farms is an association that allows people to get farming or gardening experience, as well as room and board, in exchange for a helping hand.

Join a seed savers network (like Kokopelli) to help save and exchange vintage seed outside of the commercial circuit. You can also start a local seed savers group to promote and learn how to save local varieties.

Join associations to replant tree cover, to learn about wild plants, or save habitat for wild plants and animals. There are nature programs where volunteers can go to help nesting turtles or rescue birds from oil slicks.

3) <u>Align with like minded people</u>

Take a permaculture course. Permaculture is a method of design based on the systemic understanding of ecology. It teaches how to create systems that have the diversity, adaptability and resilience of natural systems and is based on the threefold ethic of 'earth care, people care, fair share'. *8 shields healthy village building project*, incredible edibles, transition towns, global village* projects, are all permaculture-connected initiatives that you might like to investigate.

Join a charity working to relieve suffering in refugee camps, hospices, orphanages, disaster relief or working with asylum seekers. You can even start your own NGO if you a championing a cause that needs support.

Campaign for Greenpeace or anti nuclear associations in your area.

Organise workshops or conferences within your institutions or closer communities to raise awareness about peak oil, shale gas, social issues such as modern slavery, climate change, genetic engineering, nano technology, nuclear issues, and chemical pollution.

Learn about new forms of decision making and power sharing such as *Sociocracy* and discuss these ideas in open forums; put them to test in the workplace, at school or in collectives.

Learn to master skills that are rapidly disappearing and help to transmit useful heritage

Learn about new and alternative technologies that you can share.

Learn to practice alternative methods of healing and nutrition.

4) <u>Work on your inner landscape</u>

"The self is the most accessible and potentially comprehensible whole system" *[8] It is also our most important leverage point. When the self, a system within a larger system, has become disconnected from the greater whole there is dysfunctional behaviour. Reconnecting is vital and there are many ways to start off this process.

Do a meditation retreat.

Take or organise a non-violent communication course; a neurolinguistic programming workshop; a self-development course; a '*dragon dreaming*' workshop; some form of Psychotherapy or a *psych-k workshop*[9]; a 'village building' course.

Do a workshop on the '*work that reconnects*'*[10] to help you integrate the changes that we are part of and come to terms with the concerns and fears that haunt us.

These are just a few suggestions from the many similar courses and methods that are on offer to help us reconnect and reframe our paradigm.

Jessie Darlington

Our earth is like a small boat.

Compared with the rest of the cosmos, it is a very small boat and it is in danger of sinking.

We need a person to inspire us with calm confidence,

To tell us what to do.

Who is that person?

The Mahayana Buddhist Sutras tell us that you are that person.

If you are yourself, if you are at your best, then you are that person.

Only with such a person- calm, lucid, aware- will our situation improve.

I wish you good luck.

Please be yourself.

Please be that person.

Thich Nhat Hanh

Endnotes

(1) *Transition Manual.* Rob Hopkins (GreenBooks Ltd, Devon G.B. 2008)
(2) Jean Houston
(3) *Coming Back to Life.* Joanna Macy, Molly Young Brown (New Society Publishers 1998) I have readapted this story with the kind permission of Joanna Macy, following an account of an ancient Buddhist prophecy interpreted by Choegal Rinpoche of the Tashi Jong community in Northern India.
(4) Chief Seattle
(5) Thich Nhat Hanh
(6) *The Divine Matrix.* Gregg Braden (Hay House, 2007)
(7) *Inquiring Mind Vol.10 No.2 Spring 1994.* Thich Nhat Hanh
(8) *Permaculture Principles and Pathways Beyond Sustainability.* David Holmgren (Holmgren Design Services, 2002)
(9) psych-k workshops
(10) *Coming Back to Life.* Joanna Macy, Molly Young Brown (New Society Publishers 1998)

About the Author

Jessie Darlington lives, works and teaches on a thirty year old permaculture project in Southern France. She is contributing to the design of a new culture of perennity and resilience in all aspects of life and hoping to help bring about the birth of a new version of 'us' made up of all the freely contributing and diverse 'me's'. www.jessieschildrensbooks.com

Other recommended reading

The Empowerment Manual. Starhawk (New Society Publishers 2011)

The Possible Human. Jean Houston (Penguin Putnam Inc 1982)

The Biology of Belief. Bruce H. Lipton (Hay House 2015)

<u>8sheilds.org</u>

<u>newstoryhub.com</u>

"An inspiring collection of short stories that explore modern themes of ecology and spirituality through the medium of the folk tale."

Alex Walker, Findhorn Foundation Community

In a world full of bad news, false news and mind-numbing media, we need new stories that inspire. 'Transition Tales' is such a collection of short stories. New, ancient and familiar tales are re-crafted in the telling as parables for today's world, to nurture the healing potential of the human spirit and weave new dreams to envisage how things could be and our power to change how we interact with our world. Each short story only takes a few minutes to read yet encapsulates a wealth of wisdom, food for reflective thought and fodder for discussion and dialogue, suitable for all ages of readers; children, youth and adults.

– Robyn Francis, permaculture pioneer, educator and author.

Our world in transition needs inspiration to complete its metamorphosis; Cooperation, solidarity and especially the recognition that we must give to all the players in nature that constitute life on this planet. These little tales are an incitement to undertake the difficult task of transformation that must begin inside of ourselves. I am sure that these stories will inspire you to join this journey of change that will leave a better world for the children of the future.

– Bernard Alonso-coauthor of La permaculture Humaine – les cles pour vivre la transition (Human Permaculture – the keys to the Transition,) Ecosociété

Printed in the United States
By Bookmasters